WINNIPEG

WN

RARY

D0200613

Here's what kids and parents have to say to Ron Roy, author of the A to Z Mysteries series:

"I sometimes get up very early just to read one of your mystery books. They are my first favorite books."—Logan R.

"I like [your] books, because they make a lot of sense, and they are fun to try and solve."
—Zachary F.

"Every time I go to the library, I head straight for your books. I could read ten every day."
—Jennie J.

"Thanks for the great, interesting, wonderful books you write."—Graham D.

"I just CAN'T put A to Z Mysteries down!"
—Makayla W.

"Just wanted to let you know that your books are making a big impression in our house and are really helping my seven-year-old with his reading!"—Alice K.

*This book is for all my readers who have sent
me letters and e-mails. Thank you!*
—R.R.

To Yasha, my white wolf.
—J.S.G.

Text copyright © 2004 by Ron Roy
Illustrations copyright © 2004 by John Steven Gurney
All rights reserved under International and Pan-American Copyright
Conventions. Published in the United States by Random House
Children's Books, a division of Random House, Inc., New York, and
simultaneously in Canada by Random House of Canada Limited, Toronto.

www.randomhouse.com/kids
www.ronroy.com

Library of Congress Cataloging-in-Publication Data
Roy, Ron.
The white wolf / by Ron Roy ; illustrated by John Steven Gurney.
    p.   cm. — (A to Z mysteries)   "A Stepping Stone Book."
SUMMARY: While visiting their friend Wallis and her adopted daughter on
Mount Desert Island, Maine, Josh, Dink, and Ruth Rose investigate why
three white wolf cubs were stolen, and by whom.
ISBN 0-375-82480-4 (trade) — ISBN 0-375-92480-9 (lib. bdg.)
[1. Robbers and outlaws—Fiction. 2. Mount Desert Island (Me.)—Fiction.
3. Wolves—Fiction. 4. Mystery and detective stories.] I. Gurney, John, ill. II. Title.
III. Series: Roy, Ron, 1940– . A to Z mysteries.
PZ7.R8139Wf 2004   [Fic]—dc22   2003015524

Printed in the United States of America   10 9 8 7 6 5 4 3 2 1   First Edition

RANDOM HOUSE and colophon and A TO Z MYSTERIES are registered trademarks
and A STEPPING STONE BOOK and colophon and the A to Z Mysteries colophon
are trademarks of Random House, Inc.

A to Z Mysteries®

The White Wolf

by **Ron Roy**

illustrated by
John Steven Gurney

A STEPPING STONE BOOK™

Random House 🏠 New York

CHAPTER 1

"There he is!" shouted Ruth Rose. She pointed at the sky, where a small seaplane was getting ready to land.

Dink, Josh, and Ruth Rose were standing on a pier in Essex, Connecticut. It was a warm summer morning, and Ruth Rose was dressed in lavender from her headband down to her sneakers. Even her sneaker laces were lavender!

"It's so cool that planes can land on the water," Dink said. His full name was Donald David Duncan, but everyone called him Dink.

As the kids watched, the seaplane touched the top of the water. Small rainbows formed as water shot into the air. Then the plane piloted toward them.

"I see Walker!" Josh said, waving at the plane.

Walker was Wallis Wallace's brother. Wallis was a famous mystery writer. The kids had met her and Walker when they came to Connecticut. Then the kids had visited Wallis at her castle in Maine.

Walker waved back and taxied the seaplane to the end of the pier. "Hi, guys," he said, grinning. "Ready to fly?"

"We sure are!" Josh said. He, Dink, and Ruth Rose grabbed their backpacks.

"Hand me your stuff, and I'll help you climb aboard," Walker said.

A few yards away, Dink's mother tooted her car horn. Dink waved and watched his mother drive away.

When the kids were all inside the plane's cockpit, Walker showed them how to fasten their seat belts for the ride.

"This will be a short flight," Walker said when the kids were all buckled up. "We'll be in Acadia National Park before you know it. Mount Desert Island is part of the park."

"Cool!" Ruth Rose said.

"All right, here we go," Walker said. He taxied the seaplane away from the pier. In just a few seconds, they were airborne.

"We'll be flying over the water the whole way," Walker said. "You should see plenty of boats. Maybe even a whale!"

The kids kept their eyes on the water as Walker flew north. They didn't see any whales, but they did see thousands of birds and a lot of small islands.

"We're over Maine now," Walker said after about a half hour. "Mount Desert Island is right below us."

"It really looks beautiful," Dink said.

"Everything around is so green!"

"It's gigantic!" Josh said.

"It almost looks like a dinosaur's head with his mouth open," Ruth Rose commented.

"Where's your cabin?" Dink asked.

"Look right where the dinosaur's

nose would be," Walker said. He pointed out the window. "See that little harbor? It's called Seal Harbor. Our cabin is about a mile from where I'll be landing."

The plane zoomed down, then leveled off. A few minutes later, the kids felt the pontoons touch down on the water with a *swoosh*.

Walker piloted the plane toward a long wooden dock. The kids saw their friend Wallis waving at them.

Next to her on the dock was a smiling girl with long dark hair. She was sitting in a wheelchair, waving.

"Who's that with Wallis?" Ruth Rose asked.

"That's Abbi Wallace," Walker said, "Wallis's surprise for you."

CHAPTER 2

A minute later, Dink, Josh, and Ruth Rose were standing on the dock with their backpacks.

"I have to fly some fishermen and women to a camp farther north," Walker told the kids as he got back in the plane. "I'll see you guys tonight."

"Hey, welcome to Mount Desert Island!" Wallis called as she ran toward them.

"Hi, Wallis!" the kids shouted, then each gave her a hug.

"Grab your stuff and follow me," she said.

Wallis led them up the dock and stopped in front of the girl in the wheelchair. "Abbi, these are my friends from Connecticut. Dink, Josh, Ruth Rose," Wallis said, pointing to each of them, "meet my daughter, Abigail. She likes to be called Abbi, with an 'i.'"

Josh stared at Wallis. "You never told us you had a daughter!" he said.

Abbi laughed. "Mom just adopted me a few months ago," she said.

"Abbi's parents died a few years back," Wallis explained. "I heard about Abbi from a friend, so I invited her and some other kids to the castle for Christmas."

Wallis grinned at her daughter. "After knowing Abbi for only an hour, I knew I wanted her in my life permanently," she said.

"That is so awesome," Ruth Rose said. "How old are you, Abbi?"

"Almost thirteen," Abbi said. "How about you?"

"We're all almost nine," Dink put in.

Josh shook Abbi's hand. "Why are you in a wheelchair?" he asked.

"I have spina bifida," said Abbi.

"What's that?" Josh asked.

"Before I was born, when I was still inside my birth mother, my spine didn't develop right," Abbi explained to the kids. "So my legs don't work. I have to use a wheelchair most of the time."

"Well, now that you've all met, let's get home," Wallis said. "If I know these three kids, they're hungry!" She started walking toward the parking lot.

"Josh sure is," Dink teased. "His stomach was growling so loud, Walker thought there was a wolf in the plane!"

"There are wolves on this island!" Abbi said. "I've seen them through my telescope!"

"Wolves?" Josh gulped. "Really?"

Wallis stopped next to a red van. She clicked a remote, which opened a door and lowered a ramp. Abbi wheeled her chair up the ramp and into the van.

"That's so cool!" Ruth Rose said.

Wallis unlocked the other doors, and the kids piled in. Ruth Rose and Josh sat in the rear with Abbi, and Dink sat up front with Wallis.

They drove along a road lined with

tall pine trees. Through the branches, Dink caught glimpses of sky and water.

After a few minutes, Wallis pulled off the road onto a bumpy driveway. "There it is," Wallis said, pointing to a long, shady cabin. She parked next to a flagpole flying an American flag.

The low building nestled beneath sweet-smelling pine trees. Wooden steps led up to a roofed deck that circled the entire cabin. Beside the steps was a ramp that sloped up to the deck.

"I love your house!" Ruth Rose said as they got out of the van. "It's so cool and quiet here."

"I usually wheel myself up the ramp," Abbi said. "But it's more fun to have someone push me."

"I'll do it!" Josh said. He guided the wheelchair up the wooden ramp with the others following.

"Do you want to see the wolves?" Abbi asked.

"Where are they?" Josh asked. He

looked around the deck nervously.

"Over here," Abbi said. She guided her wheelchair across the deck to a telescope. "Take a look, but don't jiggle it. I have it set right on the wolf's lair."

Josh walked over to the telescope, squinted one eye, and peered into the lens. "All I see are rocks and bushes."

"Keep looking," Abbi said. "I saw the wolf just before Mom and I went to meet you guys."

Josh kept his eye on the telescope lens. Suddenly he jumped back. "Holy moly!" he shouted.

"What?" Dink said. He and Ruth Rose hurried to join Josh and Abbi at the telescope.

"I just saw a gigantic white wolf!" Josh said.

CHAPTER 3

Dink and Ruth Rose looked into the distant trees, trying to see the wolf.

"All I can see are some rocks," Dink said.

"The wolf is white, so she blends in," Abbi said. "You need the telescope."

Josh backed away, and Ruth Rose took his place at the telescope. "Oh my gosh," she breathed. "It's beautiful!"

"Can I look?" Dink asked.

Ruth Rose stepped back, and Dink peered into the telescope. "I see it!" he said.

Suddenly they heard a wolf howling. Everyone jumped, and Abbi started to laugh.

"I recorded the wolf's voice," she said. She pointed to a small tape recorder on a table. Next to it was a box of labeled cassettes.

Dink read a few of the labels: RACCOONS, FROGS, CRICKETS, SQUIRRELS, BIRDS, CHIPMUNKS.

"You recorded all these animal sounds?" Dink asked.

Abbi nodded. "It's my hobby," she said. "I've been trying to record seals, but they never seem to make noise when I'm around!"

"You have seals here?" Josh asked.

Abbi nodded. "A bunch of them live on a rocky island out there," she said, pointing toward the front of the cabin. "That's why this is called Seal Harbor."

Abbi replayed the wolf's howl.

"It sounds lonely," Ruth Rose said.

Abbi nodded. "She could be lonely," she said. "She might miss the rest of her pack."

"How do you know the wolf is a girl?" asked Dink.

Abbi grinned. "Because she has three babies!" she said.

"Let me see!" Josh said. He put his eye to the telescope again. "I don't see any babies."

"I've only seen them a couple of times," Abbi said.

Josh let Abbi have another look. "The cubs are there," she said. "They're lying right next to the mother. Their white fur blends in with hers."

Josh looked again. "Guys, I see them!" he said.

Ruth Rose, then Wallis, peered into the telescope. They grinned and said, "Ooh, aren't they cute!"

When it was Dink's turn, he laughed out loud. The plump baby wolves were

cuddled next to their mom, playing with each other's tails.

"Who wants lunch?" Wallis asked.

"I do!" said Josh.

Abbi leaned over to a panel near the door and pushed a button. Immediately the door opened inward. "Cool, huh?" she said.

"All the doors operate that way," Wallis said. "I bought this cabin because the previous owner was also in a wheelchair."

The kids followed Wallis and Abbi inside. The living room had a braided rug on the floor. All the chairs and sofas looked soft and comfortable. A stone fireplace took up nearly one wall. Shelves on both sides of the fireplace held books, board games, and seashells.

To the left of the fireplace were wide glass doors with a view of the sky, ocean, and islands.

"This place is awesome," Josh said.

"Thank you! Come on, I'll show you where you're sleeping, then we'll eat," Wallis told them.

"Ruth Rose, would you like to share my room?" Abbi asked. "You can have the top bunk."

"Great! I'll follow you," Ruth Rose said.

"You two have a treat," Wallis said to Dink and Josh. "Come on."

She led the boys out through the

glass doors. They followed her around to a different side of the deck.

"Oh my gosh!" Josh said.

A tent had been set up right on the deck, under the roof. Inside the tent were twin beds, a small table with a lamp, and a rug on the floor.

"It was Abbi's idea. She thought you'd enjoy falling asleep listening to the waves," Wallis said. "You might even hear the seals."

"It's excellent!" Dink said. "Thanks for going to so much trouble."

"No trouble at all," Wallis said. "Get settled, then come back to the kitchen when you're ready."

The boys entered the tent and chose beds. "Isn't this cool?" Dink said.

"I guess," Josh said.

"What's wrong?" Dink asked, emptying his pack onto his cot.

"What if the wolves come up here?"

Josh asked. "Or even bears?"

"Wolves and bears don't eat people, Josh," Dink said.

"Yeah, what do they eat?" Josh asked.

Just then, they heard Abbi yell from the deck. "MOM!" she shouted.

Dink and Josh pounded out of the tent and tore around the corner. They saw Abbi sitting with one eye pressed up against the telescope.

Ruth Rose and Wallis came running from the other direction.

"What's wrong, honey?" Wallis asked.

"Somebody took the baby wolves!" Abbi cried.

"Took them? What do you mean?" Wallis asked. "How could anyone take them?"

"I saw it through the telescope!" Abbi insisted. "A man and a woman grabbed the puppies!"

CHAPTER 4

Ruth Rose bent over and peered through the telescope. She shook her head. "I don't see any wolves at all," she said. "Not even the mother."

"The mother wasn't there," Abbi said. "She might have gone to look for food."

Wallis looked at Abbi. "What exactly did you see, honey?"

Abbi had tears in her eyes. "A man and a woman stuck the puppies into a cage!"

Wallis gave Abbi a hug. "Let's go inside and call the police," she said.

The four kids followed Wallis into

the kitchen. The table was set with bread, sliced meats, cheese, and a big green salad.

Wallis walked to the wall phone, where she had taped a list of emergency numbers. She dialed and waited.

"Hello, police department?" she said. "This is Wallis Wallace, on Seal Harbor. My daughter, Abbi, just witnessed three baby wolves being stolen! No, she saw it through her telescope from our cabin."

Wallis paused, said, "Thank you," then hung up. "The police are sending a game warden out to talk to you," she told Abbi.

"When?" Abbi asked. "They have to catch them fast! Those babies need their mother to feed them!"

"The officer I spoke with said the game warden would come right away," Wallis said. "So let's all have some lunch while we wait."

They were halfway through their

sandwiches when they heard a jeep pull up next to Wallis's van. A woman wearing a brown uniform stepped out. She had a badge that said GAME WARDEN over her shirt pocket.

The woman was holding a small tape recorder.

"Please come in," Wallis said. When they were all seated, the woman smiled at the kids. "I'm Nadine Banks. Which one of you is Abbi?" she asked.

"I am," Abbi said.

"Do you mind if I tape this interview?" Nadine asked. "Please tell me exactly what you saw through your telescope."

Abbi told Nadine how she had been watching the wolves ever since she discovered them a couple of weeks ago.

"It was just the mom at first," Abbi said. "Then one day, I saw the babies come out of the lair. It was so exciting!"

"I'll bet it was," Nadine said. "I knew

about the white wolf, but I didn't know she'd had puppies. Go on, Abbi."

"Then today, I was watching while my mom made lunch," Abbi said. "The mother wolf was gone for a while, and the babies were sleeping in the sun. Suddenly a man and woman grabbed the babies and stuck them in a cage!"

"Can you describe the man and woman?" Nadine asked.

"They were only there a couple of minutes," Abbi said. "They both wore T-shirts and shorts and baseball caps. But she had a long blond ponytail. It stuck out the back of her cap."

"Good. Did you notice anything else?" Nadine asked.

"No. After they put the puppies in the cage, the people left," Abbi said. "My telescope was trained just on the lair, so I couldn't see where they came from or where they went."

Nadine shut off her tape recorder.

"Taking animals out of Acadia National Park is illegal," she said. "I don't know if we'll catch these two, but we'll try. Thank you for reporting what you saw, Abbi."

Nadine left, promising to be back in touch if she learned anything.

"I wish we could do something!" Abbi said as the jeep pulled away.

"Could Walker look for the thieves from his plane?" Ruth Rose asked.

"What a great idea!" Wallis said. She picked up the kitchen phone again.

Wallis dialed, listened, then said, "Walker, this is Sis. Call home as soon as you get this message. Abbi was at her telescope, and she saw a man and woman steal those baby wolves! Both in shorts and caps. The woman had blond hair."

Wallis hung up the phone. "I got his voice mail," she said. "Don't worry, honey, your uncle is always good about checking his voice messages."

Abbi backed away from the table and wheeled herself out to the deck. Dink, Josh, and Ruth Rose helped Wallis clear the table, then walked out themselves. They found Abbi peering through the telescope.

"I saw the mother come back," Abbi said. "She sniffed the ground, then went into her lair."

"Maybe we should go out there and investigate," Ruth Rose said, looking toward the woods.

"Out where?" Josh asked.

"To the wolf's lair," Ruth Rose answered. "We might find some clues."

"Would you?" Abbi asked.

Josh froze. "Um, what if the mother wolf thinks *we* took her babies?" he said.

"Wolves are afraid of humans," Abbi told Josh. "If she sees you coming, she'll hide until you leave."

"How do we get there?" Dink asked.

Abbi pointed toward a slight clearing in the woods behind the cabin. "I think there's a sort of trail there," she said. "If you follow it uphill, it should go pretty close to where the wolves live."

"But what if the trail stops or leads somewhere else?" Josh said. "We could get lost out there."

Abbi made room for Josh at the telescope. "See that big dead tree behind the rocks?" she asked.

"Yeah, I see it," said Josh.

"If you get lost, just look up and find the tree," Abbi said. "Coming back, look for our flagpole."

"I say let's do it," Ruth Rose said. She looked at Dink and Josh.

Dink nodded.

Josh gulped. "Okay, let's hit the trail!" he said.

CHAPTER 5

The kids left the deck, passed Wallis's van and the flagpole, and walked into the trees. They turned and waved to Abbi, who waved back.

"This looks like a trail," Dink said, looking down.

The kids kept their eyes on the ground as they moved deeper into the trees. Soon Abbi and the cabin were out of sight.

The land was level for the first few minutes, then it angled sharply upward. The kids hiked in single file, with Josh leading and Dink last in line.

Fallen trees, roots poking out of the ground, and jagged rocks made walking difficult.

"I don't see any trail at all!" Josh wailed when they stopped to look around. High above their heads, tall trees blocked out the sky.

"I think we should just keep going up," Ruth Rose said. "If we get out of these trees, we might be able to see that dead one Abbi showed us."

They kept climbing. Dink could hear Josh and Ruth Rose taking deep breaths. He was sweating and swatting at mosquitoes.

After about twenty minutes, Josh stopped. "It better not be much farther," he panted.

"It's not. Look!" Ruth Rose said. She pointed uphill behind Josh.

"It's the dead tree!" Dink said. "We're almost there!"

It took them ten more minutes of climbing before they were standing at the base of the tree. Josh turned and waved his arms high in the air in case Abbi was watching.

Near the dead tree stood a pile of giant boulders. Behind the tree, the land sloped downward toward a cliff.

"It's beautiful up here," Dink said.

"You can see for miles!" Ruth Rose said. "Look how blue the water is."

"And look how dark those clouds are," Josh said nervously. "I sure don't want to be up here in a thunderstorm."

The kids split up and walked among the rocks and boulders. It took only a few seconds for Dink to find animal tracks in the sand.

"Guys, over here!" he called.

Josh and Ruth Rose found him on his knees. "Look, are these wolf tracks?"

Josh and Ruth Rose knelt next to Dink.

"They do look like pawprints," Ruth Rose said, studying the sandy ground.

Josh put his own hand next to a pawprint. "Look how big these tracks are!" he said.

Ruth Rose pointed to some shoe-prints. "Do you think these are the kidnappers' prints?" she asked.

"Maybe," Dink said. "But other people must come up here, too."

The kids prowled among the rocks. They found animal tracks, but no more from humans.

Josh stopped in front of two rock slabs leaning against each other. Beneath the rocks, a burrow had been dug, leaving a mound of loose dirt.

"Guys, I think I found the den!" Josh whispered.

The kids knelt and peered down into the dark lair.

"What if the mother wolf is down there right now?" Josh asked.

Suddenly they heard a wolf howl. All three kids jumped back.

"Run!" yelled Josh.

"She's not down there," Ruth Rose said. "Look!"

The mother wolf was standing on top of a pile of boulders about one hundred yards away. She was watching the kids with her ears standing straight up.

While the kids looked at her, she let out another howl, then leaped off the rocks and disappeared.

"What should we do?" asked Josh.

"Nothing," Dink said. "I think she's just looking for her babies."

"Let's move away from her lair in case she comes," Ruth Rose said.

Dink and Josh followed Ruth Rose. They walked toward the cliff and stood looking down at the ocean.

The ground there was too rocky to show any kind of prints.

"I wonder how that man and woman got the baby wolves out of here," Dink said.

"In a cage," Josh reminded him. "Remember what Abbi said?"

"I know, but what did they do with the cage?" Dink asked. "Cars can't drive up here, so how did they get the cage away?"

"By boat, maybe," Ruth Rose said, pointing down at the ground. "Look!"

Not five feet away from where they stood, a narrow path led down toward the water.

CHAPTER 6

"Let's check it out," Dink said, moving toward the path.

Josh and Ruth Rose followed him. The narrow track was steep, but rocks and roots provided footholds.

"Stop!" Josh shouted after they'd gone down about fifty feet.

"What?" asked Ruth Rose. She was directly behind Josh and nearly collided with his back.

"Blueberries!" Josh said. The bushes on both sides of the trail were loaded with clusters of dark blue berries. Josh reached for a branch and began picking.

"Eat some, guys," he told Dink and Ruth Rose. "They're excellent!"

But Dink was looking at the ground under their feet. Dozens of blueberries had been crushed in the dirt.

"These berries are fresh," Dink said. "Someone walked on them recently!"

"Someone like the wolf kidnappers!" Ruth Rose said. "They must have carried the cage down this way!"

"Let's keep going," Dink said.

Three minutes later, they were standing on a small beach. "A boat could land here," Dink said.

Ruth Rose looked back up at the path they'd just come down. "It would be easy," she said. "Just drag your boat up here, carry the cage up that path, and steal the puppies."

"Just about everybody out here must have a fishing boat or sailboat," Josh said.

Dink sat on the sand and gazed out at the water. "I still don't understand why anyone would want those wolves," he said.

Josh sat on one side of Dink, and Ruth Rose sat on the other. Josh's fingertips and lips were stained dark blue.

"Are wolves valuable?" Ruth Rose asked. "I mean, can you get money for them?"

Dink shrugged. "Maybe, but who would buy a baby wolf?" he asked.

Josh glanced up at the darkening sky. "We'd better head back," he said.

The kids climbed back up the trail to the clifftop. They looked around but didn't see the mother wolf again.

With dark clouds hiding the sun, the kids headed into the woods. They started walking downhill.

"Is this the right way?" Josh asked after a few minutes. "All these trees look alike."

Ruth Rose turned back around and squinted her eyes. "I can still see the dead tree," she said. She turned to face downhill. "So the flagpole should be down there somewhere."

They looked, but their eyes couldn't penetrate the thick shrubbery.

"We're lost," Josh said. "We'll be out here forever! I'll have to eat bark and twigs!"

"Maybe *you* will," Ruth Rose said. "But not me!" She picked out a tall tree

and started climbing nimbly up it.

"Where are you going?" Josh asked.

"To get a hamburger and a milk-shake," Ruth Rose said over her shoulder.

When all Dink and Josh could see were the bottoms of Ruth Rose's sneakers, she stopped climbing.

"We're not lost! I can see Wallis's flagpole!" Ruth Rose yelled down.

When Ruth Rose was back on the ground, she led them to the original trail.

Ten minutes later, they all saw the back of Wallis's cabin.

Raindrops splashed on the kids as they bounded up the cabin steps. They found Walker, Wallis, and Abbi sitting at the kitchen table.

"Hey, guys," Walker said. "Abbi told us you went to the scene of the crime."

"Without telling us," Wallis added.

"Sorry," Dink said. "But you weren't here and—"

"It's okay this time," Wallis said. "Abbi explained why you left so suddenly."

"Did you see the mother wolf?" Abbi asked.

"Yes! She was standing on some rocks howling at us, then she took off!" Josh said. "I still have goose bumps!"

The kids explained what else they'd seen.

"We think the people Abbi saw carried the cage down to the ocean. There was a little path, and blueberries that were crushed by their feet. They must have had a boat waiting!" Ruth Rose said.

"But any hiker could have crushed the berries," Wallis said. "It didn't have to be the wolf-nappers."

"How else would they get away from there with the wolves?" Abbi asked. "Are there roads up there for cars?"

"No, but there are other trails that lead to roads," Wallis said.

"And even if the thieves did use that path to get the cage to a boat, we'd never be able to prove it," Walker said. "There are hundreds of boats around these islands every day."

Walker looked at Dink, Josh, and Ruth Rose. "After I got Sis's message, I took my plane up for a look," he said. "I saw plenty of people in boats, but no cages holding baby wolves."

He put his hand over Abbi's. "I'm sorry I can't tell you more, Abbi."

Just then, they heard a toot from down by the water.

Wallis leaned over toward the sliding glass doors and waved. "That's Morris," she said. "He runs the mail boat, even in the rain."

"May I be excused?" Abbi asked. "And would someone help me move my telescope?"

"We'll help," Dink said. He, Josh, and Ruth Rose followed Abbi out to the deck. She wheeled up to the telescope.

"Where do you want it?" Ruth Rose asked.

"Out front," Abbi said. "Where I can watch the water."

She gazed up at the three kids. "Walker is right. There are zillions of boats around here," Abbi said. "But if the people who took the wolf puppies have a boat, I'll find them!"

CHAPTER 7

It took them only a few minutes to carry the telescope to the front section of the deck. Abbi showed them where to position it.

The rain drummed steadily on the tin roof over the porch.

Josh put his eye to the lens. "I can hardly see anything through the rain," he said.

"I'll have to wait till it stops," Abbi said.

Dink knew Abbi was disappointed that she couldn't use her telescope. "Do you have Monopoly?" he asked. "We could play till the rain stops."

Abbi nodded. "Sure, it's on the shelf by the fireplace."

Josh rubbed his hands together and grinned. "How about we make teams? Boys against girls?"

Abbi and Ruth Rose exchanged glances.

"You're doomed," Ruth Rose said.

The kids set up a table in the living room. Wallis and Walker joined the teams. Thunder boomed and lightning lit up the ocean as they played late into the evening.

The rain finally stopped, but the game still wasn't over when Wallis yawned and declared it bedtime.

Dink picked up a flashlight, and he and Josh walked out onto the deck. They stood for a minute and stared toward the ocean. They could hear waves hitting rocks, and the smell was sweet and salty.

"I wonder where those poor baby

wolves could possibly be," Josh said.

"And the mother," Dink added. "Gee, maybe she came down here and crawled into your bed."

Josh laughed. "Grandmother, what big teeth you have!" he said like Little Red Riding Hood.

The boys made their way around the deck and slipped inside their tent.

After they were undressed and beneath their blankets, Dink reached out and shut off the lamp. He was almost asleep when Josh grabbed his shoulder.

"Dink!" Josh whispered. "Something's moving around outside the tent!"

Dink opened his eyes. "What? All I hear is you keeping me awake."

"Shhh! Listen!" Josh hissed.

Dink yawned. "Josh, if you're . . ." Then Dink heard a slithery noise, like something scratching against canvas.

Dink gulped. Josh was right— something was outside their tent!

A moment later, he heard a wolf howling.

"Oh, gosh!" Josh cried. "The mother wolf came after us. She's on the deck!"

When the wolf howl stopped, Dink heard another strange noise—rubber wheels squeaking on the wooden deck. He also heard two girls giggling.

Dink smiled. "That wasn't a wolf," he told Josh.

"It wasn't?" Josh whispered. "What was it?"

"Something much worse than a wolf,"

Dink whispered in return, holding back a giggle.

"What could be worse?" Josh asked. "A bear?"

"Even worse," Dink said. "That's Ruth Rose and Abbi out there, trying to scare you with Abbi's wolf recording. And they did!"

"Did not," Josh said.

"Did too," Dink said, just before he fell asleep.

The next morning was bright and sunny. The only signs of the storm were a few puddles.

"What do you kids have planned?" Wallis asked at the breakfast table.

"I'm going to sit at my telescope until I find those people who took the wolf pups," Abbi said.

"We'll help her," Dink said. "We can each take turns looking through the telescope."

Wallis stood up and carried her plate to the counter. "Well, I'm going grocery shopping. Food disappears fast in this house!"

"I'm going to work on my plane," Walker said. He helped clear the table, then left through the back door.

Abbi, Dink, Josh, and Ruth Rose took turns peering at the ocean through the telescope. They saw hundreds of boats, of all sizes and colors.

Ruth Rose pointed out a woman who was sailing a small boat. She had short blond hair.

Abbi shook her head. "No, the one I saw had a ponytail," she said. "It was sticking out that little opening in the back of her baseball cap."

It was Josh's turn at the telescope. "Hey, Abbi, take a look," he said. "A woman with long blond hair is going by in a blue motorboat."

Abbi quickly took Josh's place at the

telescope. She put her eye to the lens. "That's her!" she cried. "She's even wearing the same baseball cap!"

Abbi pointed to the boat in the harbor. "Let's watch where she goes!"

They watched as the boat moved away, growing smaller in the distance.

"I've lost her," Dink said. "There are too many small boats out there."

"Well, I can still see her," Abbi said, her eye still at the telescope.

A few seconds later, Abbi backed away from the telescope. "The woman went to one of the small islands," she said. "She tied her boat up at a dock with a blue awning at the end."

Each of the kids looked through the telescope. Each could see the dock and the blue canvas.

"Now what do we do?" Ruth Rose asked.

Abbi looked at Ruth Rose. "Someone has to check out that island," she said.

CHAPTER 8

"Who?" asked Josh.

"Us! We could look for more clues," Ruth Rose said.

"How do we get out there?" Josh asked. "By swimming?"

"Morris usually comes by around nine-thirty," Abbi said. "You can hitch a ride with him. He brings hikers and bird-watchers out to the islands all the time."

Fifteen minutes later, Dink, Josh, and Ruth Rose were sitting on Wallis's dock waiting for the mail boat. Josh was carrying food in his backpack.

Ruth Rose wore a smaller pack holding Abbi's tape recorder.

"Why are we bringing the tape recorder?" Dink asked.

"Abbi said we should ask Morris to go by those rocks where the seals live," Ruth Rose said. "If we get close enough, I'm going to try to record their voices."

"There's Morris!" Dink said, standing and waving.

A white flat-bottomed boat chugged up to the dock. A man wearing a sea captain's hat waved at the kids. "Need a lift?" he asked as he pulled his boat up to the dock.

"We're friends of Abbi, sir," Ruth Rose said. "She said you might take us out to one of those small islands."

"Sure thing, and everyone hereabouts calls me Morris," the man said. "But which island? There are about thirty of them."

Dink pointed toward the island where they'd seen the woman tie her boat up to a dock. "It's one of those," he said. "The dock has a blue awning at the end."

"Yep, I know that one," Morris said. "Some rich gentleman lives out there. His estate takes up half the island!"

Morris looked at the kids. "I don't think he welcomes visitors," he said.

Josh held up his pack. "We're just going to have a picnic," he said.

"Great place for a picnic," Morris said, "as long as you stay off private property. Come aboard!"

When the kids were zipped into life vests and seated on a bench, Morris pulled away from the dock. He directed his boat toward a cluster of three small islands. Each had a different-colored awning stretched over the water at the end of a dock.

"What are the awnings for?" Josh asked.

"They protect the boats from the sun and rain," Morris explained. "You step into your boat, you don't want to sit on a hot seat, or a wet one!"

Morris headed toward the smallest of the three islands. He pulled up to the dock, and the kids stepped out of the mail boat. They dropped their packs in the shade under the blue awning. Tied to the dock was a motorboat painted the same blue.

The kids slipped out of their life vests and passed them to Morris.

"Thanks for the ride," Ruth Rose said.

Morris handed Dink a magazine and some other mail. "Would you mind leaving this inside the gate?" he asked, pointing toward the other end of the dock.

"Sure," Dink said.

"I'll swing by here for you in about a half hour," Morris said. "Can you be

finished with your picnic by then?"

"No problem!" Josh said.

Morris gunned his engine. "Okey-dokey, see you later."

The kids watched Morris pull away. Soon his boat was just a speck on the water.

The dock was quiet and cool under the awning. The only sound was made by the water gently slapping against the small blue boat.

"Now what?" asked Josh.

The kids turned away from the water. The dock was as long as two school buses. At the other end was a small sandy beach.

The whole island was covered with trees and bushes. But part of it was fenced off. Behind the fence, among tall trees and thick shrubbery, they could see a chimney and part of a roof.

"That must be where the rich guy

lives," Josh said. He glanced down at the boat. "I wonder if that blond woman lives there, too."

"We can't go inside the fence," Dink said.

"No, but we can peek through the gate when you leave the mail," Ruth Rose said.

"Let's go," Dink said, reaching down for his backpack. "We've only got a half hour."

"What's that stuff?" Ruth Rose asked, pointing to a blue smudge on the gray dock.

Ruth Rose knelt down for a closer look. She touched the smudge, then smelled the tip of her finger.

"What is it?" asked Dink.

Ruth Rose looked up at Dink and Josh. "It's blueberries!" she said.

CHAPTER 9

All three kids were on their knees studying the stain.

"You're right," Josh said. "And it looks like it came off someone's shoe."

He traced a finger around the smudge. "See, this round edge looks like part of a heelprint."

Josh looked at Dink and Ruth Rose. "Guys, someone stepped in those blueberries we saw yesterday," he said. "This could have been made by the same person!"

"Right, the people who carried the cage down to the boat!" Ruth Rose said.

Dink glanced up. "And the awning kept last night's rain from washing it away."

"Hey! What are you kids doing?" someone shouted.

Startled, the kids looked up. A tall man and woman in shorts and T-shirts were hurrying down the dock toward them. The woman's blond ponytail flopped over one shoulder.

"We . . . we wondered if we could have a picnic here," Ruth Rose said.

Josh held up his pack.

"Do you know you're on private property?" the woman asked. "How did you get here, anyway? I don't see another boat."

"The mailman dropped us off," Ruth Rose said. "He'll be back to get us in a half hour."

Dink held out the mail. "Morris asked me to put this inside your gate," he said.

"Thanks." The man took the mail and opened the magazine.

"Okay, the boss is away, so I guess you can have your picnic," the woman said. She pointed toward the sandy beach. "Up there, please."

The man and woman turned and strode back up the dock. The kids scrambled after them.

When they reached the sand, the man walked through the gate, still reading his magazine.

"Please don't leave any litter behind," the woman said. Then she stepped inside the gate, slammed it shut, and walked through the shrubbery.

"They could be the wolf-nappers!" Ruth Rose said. "That woman had a blond ponytail!"

"When we get back, we can call the game warden!" Dink said.

"Guys, we only have a half hour," Josh declared. "Let's eat!" He sat in the sand and opened his pack.

Dink and Ruth Rose knelt as Josh brought out three juice cartons, a bag of cookies, and some grapes. High over their heads, a few gulls soared.

"Look at all those seagulls," Ruth Rose said. "Watch out, Josh, they might zoom down and grab your cookie."

"They'd better not," Josh said, glancing at the sky.

"Why don't you turn on Abbi's tape recorder?" Dink said. "If they come closer, we can get some gull noises for her collection."

"Good idea." Ruth Rose took the tape recorder out and set it on her flattened pack. She pushed the RECORD button.

The kids began to eat. The only sounds were their munching and a few gull cries.

"Guys, what are we going to do?" Ruth Rose asked. "If those are the people Abbi saw, the wolf pups could be here on this island!"

Dink turned and looked through the fence into the thick shrubbery. "But we can't get in," he said.

Ruth Rose shook her head. "Why would anyone want baby wolves?" she asked. "I just don't get it."

"The rich guy who owns this place must be their boss," Josh said. "He might have told them to steal the babies."

"But *why*?" Ruth Rose asked.

"For pets," Josh said. "I read about a movie star who had a leopard."

"But that's cruel!" Ruth Rose said. "Wild animals should be left in the wild. And those babies should be with their mother. We have to rescue them!"

"How, Ruth Rose?" Dink stood up and walked over to the gate. He tried to open it. "Locked," he muttered.

Suddenly a bunch of gulls swooped down and landed on the sand.

"Shoo!" Josh yelled, making the gulls take off again.

Just then, they heard a toot.

"There's Morris," Josh said.

The mail boat was still a ways off, chugging toward the island. The kids packed their stuff and hurried onto the dock.

They stood waiting next to the blue motorboat. Josh glanced down. Suddenly he lay flat on his belly and leaned over the boat.

"What are you doing?" Dink asked.

"Looking for clues," Josh said. "If the baby wolves were in this boat, there might be some hairs."

He peered beneath a seat. "Aha!"

Josh reached under the seat, then yelled. He jumped to his feet, shaking his hands in disgust.

"What did you see?" Ruth Rose asked.

"A mouse!" Josh said.

"Really?" Ruth Rose said. "We should catch it and set it free on land!"

"Too late," Josh said. "It's all wet and slimy and dead."

CHAPTER 10

"I gave the mail to a man," Dink said as they pulled away from the dock a few minutes later.

"Thanks a lot," Captain Morris said. "That'd be Greg Dack. He and his sister, Lynda, take care of the place for the owner."

"Do they have any pets?" Josh asked, sliding a look at Dink and Ruth Rose.

Morris shook his head. "Not that I've seen." Then he grinned. "Course, with that jungle they live in, they could hide an *elephant* on that island!"

A few minutes later, he pulled the

mail boat up to Wallis's dock.

"Thanks a lot!" the kids all said.

"My pleasure," Morris said. "Give Wallis and Walker and Abbi a big howdy from me."

"We will," Dink said. "Bye, Captain Morris!"

Morris tooted his horn and pulled away. The kids ran up the dock and into the cabin.

Wallis, Walker, and Abbi were waiting for them.

"How was your picnic?" Wallis asked. "Or should I say, how was your snooping expedition?" she added slyly.

"Did you find the wolf pups?" Abbi asked.

"No, but we might have found a clue!" Josh said. He told them about the blueberry stain on the dock. "It looked like it came off someone's shoe. Like whoever crushed those blueberries on that path!"

"Josh, anyone could have left a blueberry stain on that dock," Wallis said. "This is blueberry-picking season. We have no proof it was the people who took the wolves."

Ruth Rose told them about the brother-and-sister caretakers. "Lynda Dack has long blond hair!" she said.

"I knew it!" Abbi said.

"There was a high fence all around the place," Dink said. "We couldn't see anything inside."

Ruth Rose remembered the tape. "Abbi, we forgot to ask Morris about the seals, but we tried to tape some seagulls for you."

Ruth Rose put the tape recorder on the table and pressed the PLAY button.

At first they heard only hissing, then the sound of gulls.

Then the gull cries were interrupted by Dink, Josh, and Ruth Rose talking.

Suddenly they heard Josh's voice yell, "Shoo!"

"This is when the gulls landed near us," Ruth Rose said. "I think they wanted our food."

"It was nice of you to make the tape," Wallis said.

"But those weren't all gull sounds!" Abbi said. She rewound the tape and hit PLAY again. "Listen," she said, leaning toward the machine and turning up the volume. The others leaned in, too.

The cries were louder now. "There! Those aren't gulls," Abbi said. "I think they're the wolf pups!"

"Honey, those sound like seagulls," Wallis said. "Are you sure you're not just—"

"I know what gulls sound like," Abbi said. "I have them on another tape. It's

on the deck, the cassette marked BIRDS."

Walker hurried out to the deck and came back with the cassette. He ejected the one in the recorder and slid in the BIRDS tape.

They heard the hooting of an owl, some loons, and finally a raucous, high-pitched squawking.

"Those are gull calls," Abbi said. "Do you hear the difference?"

"Play the other one again," Ruth Rose said.

Abbi switched cassettes, and they once more heard the sounds that Abbi said were the pups.

"It *does* sound like puppies whimpering," Josh said. "My dog makes that noise when he's hungry!"

"But how did we get the wolf pups on tape?" Dink asked. "We never saw them."

"They must be hidden somewhere out there," Abbi said. "You might have heard them, but you thought they were seagull noises. Now we can tell the police!"

"But this tape doesn't prove the wolves are on that island," Walker said. "The Dacks might have dogs."

"But I saw the woman in the boat!" Abbi insisted. "I can tell the police she was the same woman I saw take the pups."

"You saw her from a long distance both times," Walker told his niece. "You might have seen two different women with long blond hair."

"Uncle Walker is right, hon," Wallis said. "We can call the game warden again, but I have a feeling she'll want more proof before she accuses those people."

"Abbi, what do wolves eat around here?" Dink asked suddenly.

Abbi looked at Dink. "Small animals, mostly," she said. "Why?"

"Well, Josh found a dead mouse

in their boat," Dink explained.

"Right, and I touched it," Josh said. "It was wet and slimy and gross!"

"You should have heard Josh scream, Abbi," Ruth Rose said.

Suddenly Abbi backed her wheelchair away from the table. She wheeled herself to the fireplace and came back with a book in her lap.

With the others watching her, she flipped some pages, then started reading:

A large part of a wolf's diet is rodents, mostly mice. Adult wolves often vomit up partially digested mice as food for their young.

Abbi closed the book. "I think those baby wolves were in that boat," she declared. "The mother wolf probably caught the mouse for her babies, and one of them was eating it when they got thrown in the cage."

"So the mouse *was* a clue!" Josh said.

"It's almost like connecting dots to make a picture," Dink said. "First Abbi saw two people steal the puppies. Then we saw human footprints near the wolves' den. Ruth Rose found a trail down to the beach and blueberry stains on the dock. And Josh found a dead mouse in the boat."

"And we heard the whimpering noises on the tape," Abbi added.

"Okay, I have to admit that I see a picture forming," Wallis said. "But what we believe isn't necessarily the truth."

"Right," Walker said. "There are a couple more dots to connect. Like how do we prove that whimpering on the tape came from the baby wolves?"

"I have an idea," Josh said quietly.

CHAPTER 11

"Tell us, Josh," Wallis said.

"I was thinking about the mother wolf," Josh said. "She would know if those were her babies whimpering on the tape."

Everyone stared at Josh.

"I don't get it," Dink said.

"I do!" Ruth Rose cried. "We let the mother wolf listen to the tape, right, Josh?"

Josh nodded. "Yeah, we can take the tape recorder to her den and play it. If the mother wolf is there, she should do something when she hears her babies crying."

"If those really are her babies on the tape," Wallis reminded them.

"There's only one way to find out," Walker said. "Come on, kids!"

Dink, Josh, Ruth Rose, and Walker left the cabin and hiked into the woods.

Ruth Rose carried Abbi's tape recorder and a copy of the tape in her backpack. Walker had slung his camera around his neck.

"I sure hope this works," Dink said as they trekked through the trees.

"Me too," Walker said. "Abbi will be heartbroken if we don't get those wolf pups back with their mother."

They stopped talking when they saw the tall dead tree. Dink, Josh, and Walker found a place to stay out of sight.

Ruth Rose set the tape recorder on the ground about fifty feet from the lair. She pressed PLAY, then ran to where the others waited.

Seconds later, they heard the taped whimpering noises. All four watchers had their fingers crossed.

Suddenly a white blur shot out of the rock cave. The mother wolf hurled herself at the tape recorder. Lying on her stomach, she made her own whimpering sounds. She put her nose next to the tape recorder, as if trying to smell her babies.

Walker was recording it all on his digital camera.

After a moment, the whimpering noises stopped, and the kids' conversation came from the tape.

The mother wolf leaped to her feet, and her ears went straight up. She barked at the tape recorder as if it were alive.

Walker motioned that they should leave, and the four backed away. When they were on the trail toward home, they stopped and high-fived each other.

"Did you see her?" Josh asked. "If that isn't proof, I don't know what is!"

"And Walker got it all on camera!" Ruth Rose said.

"I sure hope Abbi was watching," Dink said. "Will she be mad that we left her tape recorder up there?"

Walker laughed. "She'll forgive us," he said. "Between your tape and these pictures, I'm pretty sure the game warden will agree to take a boat ride out to talk to the Dacks."

Abbi and Wallis were waiting on the deck when the kids and Walker emerged from the woods.

"We saw it all!" Abbi cried. "I told you those were wolf whimpers!"

Walker grinned. "You were right on, honey," he told Abbi. "We had to leave your tape recorder up there, though."

"It was so cool," Josh said. "That mother wolf practically crawled inside the tape recorder."

"Now can we call the police and have them arrested?" Abbi asked.

"Now we can ask Nadine to pay those people a visit," Wallis said.

Nadine showed up twenty minutes later with another game warden named Jason. They borrowed Walker's camera and motored toward the island with the blue awning.

The four kids waited on the dock. To kill time, they counted all the boats they could see. The boys got a point for each motorboat, and the girls for each sailboat.

The girls were ahead eighteen sailboats to eleven motorboats when Ruth Rose screamed, "HERE THEY COME!"

Sure enough, Nadine was sitting in the bow of the boat as Jason guided it toward the dock. In the middle of the boat was a lump covered with an old blanket.

"Did you get them?" asked Abbi as Nadine stepped onto the dock.

"Piece of cake," Nadine said.

CHAPTER 12

"The puppies are pretty scared," Nadine said. She and Jason carried the bulky, covered cage up to the deck.

They set the cage in the shade. The baby wolves whimpered through the blanket.

Wallis and Walker joined them on the deck. They were both grinning.

"Can we peek in?" asked Abbi.

"Okay, but just for a second," Nadine said. "Jason and I have to get them back to their mother as soon as possible."

Nadine lifted a corner of the blanket,

and everyone peeked into the cage. The three baby wolves were huddled together. Small black eyes peered back at the kids.

"They are so amazing!" Josh said.

"They look thirsty," Abbi said. "Should we give them some water?"

"Sure, and I could use a glass, too," Jason said.

"Let's all go inside," Wallis said.

When the wolves had been given a bowl of water, the two game wardens told what happened on the island.

"At first the Dacks denied everything," Nadine said. "But then I showed them your digital pictures, and that did it. They took us to a small shed, and there were the baby wolves, crying and scared."

"Did they say why they took the wolves?" Ruth Rose asked.

Jason nodded. "It seems that Greg Dack read an ad in a magazine from some guy who wanted to buy wolves to use as watchdogs," he said. "The Dacks stood to make several thousand dollars on this little scheme."

"And right in the middle of their confession, their boss walked in," Nadine said. "He fired the Dacks on the spot. Jason called the authorities, and they'll be arrested within an hour.

Those two won't be kidnapping any more wolves."

Nadine smiled at Abbi. "If it hadn't been for you, they would have gotten away with it," she said. "And who knows what might have happened to those pups."

Nadine took a small book from her back pocket. She opened the book in front of Abbi. "This shows all the animals that live in this park," she said. "Since you have a telescope, you could help us out by letting us know how many you see."

Abbi accepted the book and beamed. "Thank you!"

Jason stood up. "Let's get those pups back to their mom," he said.

With the kids watching, Jason and Nadine carried the covered cage into the woods.

Twenty minutes later, Dink looked

up from the telescope. "They made it!" he said.

Taking turns, the kids watched the game wardens set the cage in front of the lair. They removed the blanket, unlatched the door, then backed away.

In seconds, the white mother wolf appeared. The three baby wolves scampered out of the cage and jumped on their mother. She licked them all over, then led them down into the lair.

Later, after a big dinner with blueberry pie for dessert, Dink and Josh lay in their beds.

"My stomach is going to bust," Josh moaned.

"Thanks for the warning," Dink said. "Who told you to eat three pieces of pie?"

"Oh, don't even say the word 'pie'!" Josh said.

"Pie, pie, pie!" Dink said.

A minute later, Josh said, "Dink? I heard something outside the tent. I'll bet it's Ruth Rose and Abbi trying to scare us again."

Dink crept out of his bed and peeked through the tent flap. Then he crawled back under his covers.

"Did you see them?" Josh whispered.

"I saw something about seven feet tall, covered with brown fur," Dink said. "Sweet dreams, Josh."

"You're kidding me, right?" Josh asked. "Dink? It's a joke, right? Dink?"

Dink smiled and went to sleep.

A to Z Mysteries®

Dear Readers,

Last year, I received an e-mail from a boy telling me about his sister, Abigail Vance. Abigail has spina bifida, which is a birth defect. Spina bifida happens while the baby is still inside the mother, before he or she is born.

What causes spina bifida? Doctors have learned that this birth defect occurs when the spine does not close properly, leaving the spinal cord exposed. Doctors are still learning *why* the spines of some babies do not close properly.

Spina bifida happens rarely, but it can cause nerve damage and paralysis. Abigail is paralyzed from the knees down and uses a wheelchair. When a baby is born with spina bifida, doctors can perform surgery to close the opening and preserve existing nerves.

After reading the e-mail, I called

Abigail's parents and asked them if I could put Abigail in my next book. They asked Abigail, and she said yes! So in *The White Wolf* there is a girl named Abbi. She

Abigail and Patrick Vance

uses a wheelchair because she was born with spina bifida. I know you will like Abbi, and I hope you enjoy reading *The White Wolf*.

Happy reading!

Sincerely,

Ron Roy

P.S. Please pay a visit to my Web site at www.ronroy.com!

Collect clues with Dink, Josh, and Ruth Rose in their next exciting adventure,

THE X'ED-OUT X-RAY

"My lion is faster than your dragon!" Josh shouted at Dink.

Just then Dink heard yelling from over by the stage. He tried to see what was going on, but a kid on a pink elephant blocked his view.

The yelling continued, and Dink still couldn't see. Holding on to his safety pole, he kneeled on the dragon's back for a better view.

But the dragon was slippery, and Dink suddenly felt himself falling.

Discover the Adventurous and Addictive A-List!

If you enjoyed this book, check out the other books in the A-List series.

☐ The Spy Who Barked #1   ☐ Operation Spy School #4
☐ London Calling #2   ☐ Moose Master #5
☐ Swimming with Sharks #3   ☐ Code Word Kangaroo #6

A to Z Mysteries

☐ The Absent Author   ☐ The Missing Mummy
☐ The Bald Bandit   ☐ The Ninth Nugget
☐ The Canary Caper   ☐ The Orange Outlaw
☐ The Deadly Dungeon   ☐ The Panda Puzzle
☐ The Empty Envelope   ☐ The Quicksand Question
☐ The Falcon's Feathers   ☐ The Runaway Racehorse
☐ The Goose's Gold   ☐ The School Skeleton
☐ The Haunted Hotel   ☐ The Talking T. Rex
☐ The Invisible Island   ☐ The Unwilling Umpire
☐ The Jaguar's Jewel   ☐ The Vampire's Vacation
☐ The Kidnapped King   ☐ The White Wolf
☐ The Lucky Lottery

ANDREW LOST

☐ Andrew Lost on the Dog #1   ☐ Andrew Lost in the Whale #6
☐ Andrew Lost in the Bathroom #2   ☐ Andrew Lost on the Reef #7
☐ Andrew Lost in the Kitchen #3   ☐ Andrew Lost in the Deep #8
☐ Andrew Lost in the Garden #4   ☐ Andrew Lost in Time #9
☐ Andrew Lost Under Water #5

Available wherever books are sold.
www.randomhouse.com/kids

All New!

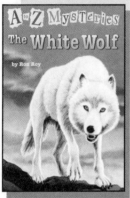

A to Z Mysteries®

A to Z Mysteries
The X'ed-Out
X-Ray
by Ron Roy

The mystery endz here...

X

A to Z Mysteries
The Yellow Yacht
by Ron Roy

Y

April 2005!

A to Z Mysteries
The Zombie Zone
by Ron Roy

Dink, Josh, and Ruth Rose are
reaching the end of the alphabet!
Can you solve all of the mysteries
before the letters run out?

Z

Collect them all, from A to Z!

STEPPING STONES®
a chapter book
Mystery

AVAILABLE WHEREVER BOOKS ARE SOLD.

www.randomhouse.com/kids

RHCB